SNOWBEAR'S CHRISTMAS COUNTDOWN

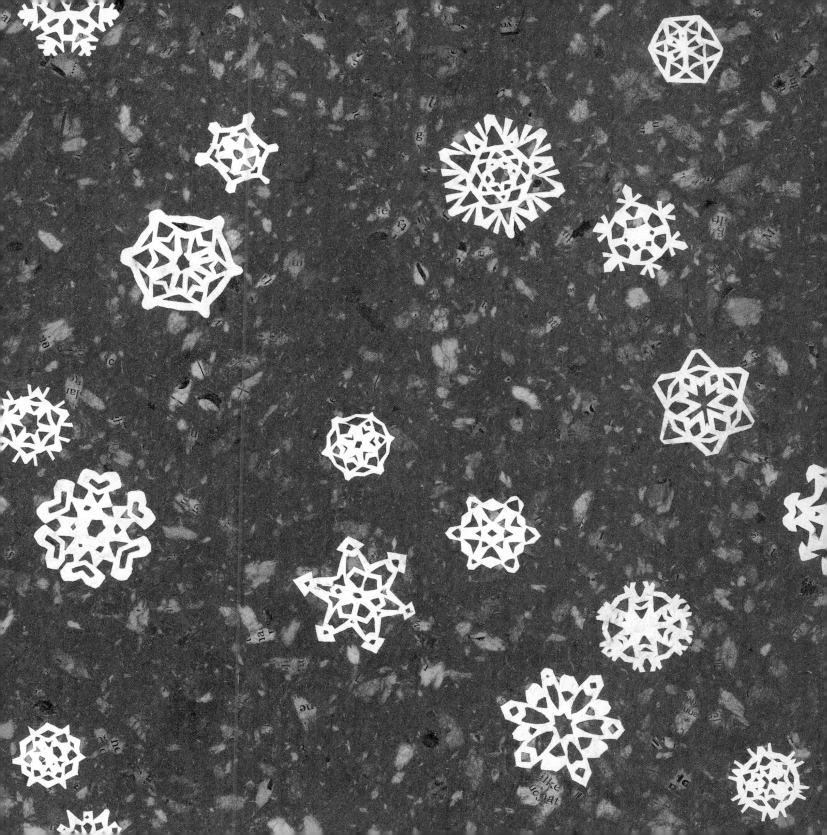

To my son, Ryan, the best gift I ever received,
and in memory of his Nana, my mother—
who always made the days leading up to Christmas
the very best times of the year — T. S.

Copyright © 2004 by Theresa Smythe. All rights reserved. Published by Scholastic Inc.,
557 Broadway, New York, NY 10012, by arrangement with Henry Holt and Company, LLC.
SCHOLASTIC and associated logos are trademarks and/or registered trademarks of Scholastic Inc.
12 11 10 9 8 7 6 5 4 3 2 1   5 6 7 8 9 10/0
Printed in the U.S.A.   40
First Scholastic printing, November 2005
The artist used cut-paper collage to create the illustrations for this book.
Designed by Amy Manzo Toth

Theresa Smythe

SNOWBEAR'S
CHRISTMAS COUNTDOWN

SCHOLASTIC INC.

New York Toronto London Auckland Sydney
Mexico City New Delhi Hong Kong Buenos Aires

It was the month of December and time for Snowbear to get ready for Christmas.

On the **1**st day he wrote a list of all the presents he wanted Santa to bring him.

Dear Santa,
Here's my list
because I've been
pretty good.
ice cream maker
snowshoes
bee hive
telescope
paints
skis
computer
thanks @
snowbear

Santa Claus
101 Candy Cane Lane
North Pole

Gran,

On the **2**nd day he took his favorite wool
hat and scarf out of the storage closet
and checked them for moth holes.

On the **3**rd day he strung a cord of brightly colored lights along the roof.

On the **4**th day he arranged his collection
of snow globes on the mantel.

On the **5**th day he wrote and mailed all of his Christmas cards.

HONEY

ADDRESSES

Charlie
9 Winter Way
Snowville

On the **6**th day he shoveled a path from his house because it had snowed the night before.

On the **7**th day he made a snowman.

On the **8**th day he made ornaments
out of paper, glitter, and glue.

glitter glitter

On the **9**th day he picked out a Christmas
tree and brought it home to decorate.

On the **10**th day he set up his toy trains.

On the **11**th day he went Christmas shopping.

On the **12**th day he wrapped all his presents for his family and friends.

On the **13**th day he went sledding down
the giant hill near his house.

On the **14**th day he caught a
cold and had to stay in bed.

cough
syrup

On the **15**th day he watched his favorite holiday movies and snuggled under the blankets.

On the **16**th day he cracked nuts
with his new nutcracker.

On the **17**th day he hung
a wreath on his door.

On the **18**th day he bought a poinsettia
plant to brighten up the kitchen.

On the **19**th day he had Charlie over for lunch.

On the **20**th day he ate too many
candy canes and got a bellyache.

On the **21**st day he went caroling with his friends.

On the **22**nd day he went ice-skating
and counted the stars.

On the **23**rd day he hung up his
stocking and read a book by the fire.

On the **24**th day it was Christmas Eve, so he made a plate of cookies for Santa and his reindeer.

FROSTING

And on the **25**th day, with the help of all his friends, he had himself a very **Merry Christmas!**